ARE YOU AFRAID OF EXAMINATIONS

ARE YOU AFRAID OF EXAMINATIONS

•

k k vasu

•

translation
dr. anishia jayadev

•

first chintha edition
july 2017

•

published
chintha publishers, thiruvananthapuram

•

typesetting
star communications, thiruvananthapuram

•

•

cover
midas

•

Distribution
DESHABHIMANI BOOKHOUSE
H O Thiruvananthapuram 695035
Email: chinthapublishers@gmail.com
Website: www.chinthapublishers.com

Branch
Head Office Kunnukuzhi • Statue Thiruvananthapuram • KSRTC Bus
Station Alappuzha • KSRTC Bus Station Ernakulam • Machingal Lane
Thrissur • IG Road Kozhikode • Mavoor Road Kozhikode • NGO
Union Building Kannur • Central Bus Terminal Complex Thavakkara
Kannur

CO - 2536 / 4374
ISBN - 978-93-86637-05-5

ARE YOU AFRAID OF EXAMINATIONS

K K Vasu

Translation
Dr. Anishia Jayadev

CHINTHA PUBLISHERS
Thiruvananthapuram 695 035

K K Vasu

K K Vasu was born in a remote village in Kerala as the eldest of nine siblings. His father Krishnan Ezhuthachan was a poor farmer and his mother Lakshmi Amma nearly illiterate. Young Vasu grew up like his brother Raman solitary and dreamy in the company of the haunting melodies of forests.

He passed the pre-university exam of Madras University and obtained first rank from the Thrissur centre. Later he specialized in Electrical Engineering. Electrical Design and control system.

He is the author of more than fifty works on literature and engineering.

He has been honoured with awards like the Sahitya Academy Award, the NCERT National award, topmost award from the Govt. of India (Rs. 1 lakh), International Book Fare award, Sahitya Pravarthaka Sahakarana sangham award, Kerala State Award, Balasahitya Academy Award, Rajana prize for short story, Bhima Award, P T Bhaskara Panikkar Award, Sahridaya Vedi Award, Pariyaram Mahatma Society Award and the Jeevana Award in literature.

He has designed, written and presented more than 500 T V films which were telecast on Doordarshan, Kerala Govt. Channel and on Satellite Channels, respectedly. His films won Kerala State Children's Film Festival award and Electronic Media Award.

He has also won Energy Conservation Award of the Kerala Government.

He designed, Built and successfully commissioned the C P (Control Pannel) of the first off shore wave Energy project of the world with the help of IIT Madras.

Content

Publishers note

$\mathbf{A}$ll those who write examinations would not win. Among those who win, students are rated into different classes of achievement. Victory in examination almost ensures victory in life. How? Bernard Shaw can be quoted at this instance. "At first we have to identify what we can do at our best. Then try to do it perfectly."

Thus the way in which one prepare for and write examinations become extremely significant. So What are the factors which are to be kept in mind while preparing for an examination?

The book *Are you afraid of examinations* attempts to answer the above question. It is the translater version of the much acclaimed Malayalam book by K K Vasu, the *Padippilum Pareekshayilum* Dr. Anishia has presented it in English lightly and lucidly.

Please accept it.

Chintha Publishers

1
How to prepare for exams

Why do we study, especially when exam comes? To win, is it not? But does all those who write exams win? And among those who win, kids are rated into different classes of achievement. Victory in an exam, many a times ensures victory in life. When we think about the secret of success in human life, Bernard Shaw can be quoted. He said, "at first we have to identify what we can do at our best. Then try to do it perfectly." This is applicable to success in examination also.

Among good friends, one may, in future become a man of good stature while the other one would be struggling to make his two ends meet. Mostly this would result from their success in the exams they appeared for in their youth. So the way in which one prepares for and writes the exam become extremely significant. And here emerges the thought about what are the factors which are to be kept in mind while preparing for an exam.

It is absolutely necessary to introspect. The idea is to understand whether you have the right attitude towards study when you start preparing for the public exam especially during the study leave. There are many reasons for a candidate to get disinterested in exams. If you are not mentally prepared, it is ideal to wait for the next chance. Or else, you will be mimicking the story of the hungry goat who wanders here and there eating irregularly. Planning is absolutely necessary for you to be successful in exams. It should also be kept in mind that if you lose one chance it doesn't matter, but you lose your chance for ever, it matters a lot.

Never learn intermittently, because, it will lead to failure. Even though it is a test on the objective mode, it is not advisable to study bit by bit, as it will not relate or stick into our memory. Years back, when exams were more of descriptive in nature, some candidates, especially those who could not afford a systematic study for want of infrastructure, tried their luck by gambling over. At times gambling work, but, in such cases, more probability is for failure. Both in mathematics and science, where the subject matter is a continuum, it should be done systematically. Never try to break the continuum. Pictures are of great importance. Some pictures may be of explanatory in nature. Some others will form answers to questions. Hence it is extremely important to learn pictures also. Drawing pictures is also needed. Pictures could form part of an answer of descriptive nature. Have you not heard picture speaks more than words? a picture is worth a thousand words? There might be examiners who may be impressed to see picturization in the answer papers. It may ever fetch better marks. Some subjects are to be learnt by writing it down several times: especially mathematics. It has to be done repeatedly.

While you learn, learn spellings by heart. This is applicable for both Malayalam, English or any other language. Now a day's, thrust is not given to learning of spelling which has deteriorated the quality of language learning. This affects learning of any subjects. Spelling is learnt best by both reading aloud and jotting it down many times.

Beforehand, the candidate should prepare himself with the most probable questions. Special effort is to be made to identify the best answer by referring to different books pertaining to same portion.

Moreover along with learning a portion, a comprehensive short note of it is also to be made. A best student learns this way. It will also enable the student to make his effort before the exam much easy. He needs to refer only the abridged note of the important portions he prepared earlier. Any one will be able to prepare a comprehension only when he understands the subject thoroughly. There are people who use symbols and numbers as short hand or creating a simple language of oneself for preparation of notes. Extra reading could be preceeded by such note taking. This is of utmost importance. The mentality of the student is extremely important while he/she is studying. One should be energetic, enthusiastic and courageous. More over, confidence is also a must. If you lack confidence, fear will brood on your mind. You may become lethargic and tired. Then you could infer what would happen to your studies. So keep it in mind that victory is only for those who are confident and courageous. There is no pointing in building up tension. When you feel like sleeping, sleep well, especially the night before exam. One who believes in god could always give their prayer to keep oneself cool. This will facilitate better control over writing exam.

2

At times it becomes difficult to study well for exams. Why?

The only reason is because you have not made studies your habit. It is repeated effort that makes you excel in studies. For this your body and mind should be attuned. Both should work together. Or else your effort will go in vain, whatever be the time you spend for your studies.

You can learn at home or at school. Whereever you learn, you should be in control of all your senses. Rather you should try to incorporate all your senses in to the process of learning. It can be better explained using an example.

Usually how do we learn? By reading aloud, or from the teaching and explanation by the teacher. Imagine we hear our teacher explaining the characteristic features of an animal. While it continues, some may feel sleepy, some may get bored. Here the only sense that takes part in study is the ears. It is only hearing that takes place. But, if the teacher shows the animal about which he is teaching, or else, the student is imagining that animal or watching a picture of it, then the eyes are also engaged. If that animal licks you, then your skin is also involved. If it would discharge some scent, then your nose will also get lined up for facilitating the study to a greater extend. That learning you will never forget. Because, instead of one sense, couple of other sense organ has also in field for making your studies perfect. So, whatever you learn, sticks to your thought and memory in a better way.

That is why you have to motivate all your senses for study. If you learn about the internal structure of a fish why not you dissect fish which was purchased at home for curry? Why don't you touch a flower, sense its smell, plant a seed and see its growth etc.

What is to be inferred from this is that you should train your learning habit incorporating better use of your sense organs.

That seems to be sensible, isn't it?

3
Precautions to be taken for writing an exam

1. While learning learn in depth. For this experimentations would aid.

2. Concentration should be sharpest so that all the attention will be on learning. For this rigorous training is needed.

3. Control all the sense organs. Control appetite. Eat healthy food. Control hearing; don't engage yourself in silly conversations. Don't answer to questions which are not asked to you. Control your sight. While reading, let your eyes not stray.

4. No need to fear, let your mind be free.

5. Control your thoughts; don't permit pessimistic thoughts to enter into. Positive thought is essential.

6. Enhance your mental power, it will enhance your memory.

7. Manage stress. Yoga and meditation are ways in which you can reduce the strain of daily life. Experienced people say that yoga soothes mind and increases concentration.

Meditation is always wrongly associated with religious practices. Atheists can also observe meditation and get themselves comforted. For meditation, adopt the padmaasana posture. For this squat, i.e. sit on the floor, right leg should be over the left thigh and vice versa. Arrange the legs in such a way that heals touch lower abdomen. This is padmasana. If this is difficult, either just squat on the floor, or sit in knees. If that is difficult, sit on a good chair. Concentrate. For this either you can identify with almighty if you are a believer. Or else you can concentrate on a spot in your body or external to you towards your front. A lighted candle or a beautiful picture can also serve the purpose. Then half close your eyes. Still try to concentrate. Half closure of eyes is suggested to prevent your environment to steal your concentration. If you close your eyes fully, sleep may defeat you.

Once you do this, make your body parts relax. Fist leg, then arms, hand, stomach, nose, ear, and eye. Then try to concentrate, continue this for half an hour. At first it will not be very easy, like a grasshopper your mind may hopp from one thing to the other, but by repeated effort you will be able to control yourself. The peace and happiness that you get from the process would be unexplainable.

As it is explained in Bhagavat Geetha,

Yatho yatho nischarathi manaschanchala masthiram

thathasthatho niyamyai thadaathmanyeva vasam nayeth

This means, the mind should be restrained and directed towards the Self, pulling the fickle and restless mind from wherever it wanders.

It is also said "atma samstham manah krithvaa na kinchit apichinthayet"-- after fixing the mind unto the Self, do not think.

In the edited volume 'Relax' by Johan White and James Fadiman, the same idea is emphasised.

8.   Notes could be prepared both at home and at class. By this we make use of two of our sense organs, the skin (fingers) and eyes. When we see what we write, it facilitate learning and increases memory. It prevents day dreaming too.

Tips for a better study

1.   Make short notes

2.   Whenever you read, have a pen or pencil in your hand,

researchers say, it adds to your concentration. When your mind starts wandering, it will keep your alert.

3. When you learn, at home take the same seat and have a specific timing. Then it will sooner become your habit. Have you not heard the statement "from womb to tomb?" it will stick on to you unto the last.

4. Seek a peaceful and quiet place where no one disturbs you. Keep away from where radios and televisions are kept. Move away from any type of such distractions and group discussions.

5. While the school is functioning, at least 45-65 hours should be allotted for studies.

6. Comforts should be minimum. Your seating should not be as cozy as to invite sleep.

7. Room should be well lit but not glaringly bright.

8. If some portion seems to be increasingly difficult, it may not necessarily be your fault. You can do some cross references in library books. The real reason may be some kind of structural anomaly that happens during writing of the matter.

9. Along with reading, frame questions and find out its answers. Underline the most important portions.

10. To make your study more fruitful, and for clarity, refer to as much of books as possible.

4

Is study a burden?

Have you not heard kid's complaining like that? Yes. But is learning that much difficult? No. Just as we breathe and eat, learning is something which we have to conduct as long as we stay healthy in this world. Only through study, we can search and know about things. It makes ourself internally rich and happy. So, study, is never a burden.

Exam is not a boring or laborious task. It is only a test of our expertise, knowledge and intelligence. It is a boon that we could learn and write exams. Do you know there are a thousand kids who does not have such a fortune? Have you not heard about kids who have to toil themselves in fields, factories, hotels etc., to make a living for them and to support their family? You might also have seen the disaster victims who have not only lost their right to learning, but all their belongings. Do you know the number of child labourers in our country? They are holding much heavier a burden that they can carry. The statistics given as a result of a study conducted by the Labour Bureau of India shows light into the lives of an alarming number of school children taking themselves to some productive job. At times the jobs are risky and demanding so that, further development of the kid becomes impossible.

At a time when the kids should play and study, they are struggling with work. Across the world, out of five hundred and twenty lakh child labourers, nearly three hundred and seventy lakh are Asian and out of them nearly one third are Indian kids. On an average, their working hours are 15 per day. How devastating! For adults, working hours are only 8.

Even in Kerala, there is child labour. With all our advancements in the field of education we are not able to control the situation. In fish pealing factory here, minimum working hours for kids is fifteen. In Delhi, as waiters and cleaners in hotel, they work for about 14 hours.

Even if they work for long, the wage they get is meager. Per day it is only below five rupees. In the cotton mills of Maharashtra the per-day wage is only 2 rupees, can you believe?

In the textile manufacturing centers of Coimbatore, thousands of kids are engaged in various jobs. Most of them help tailors in stitching cloths. Their wage is below two rupees. When the offer would be in a contract like a fixed prize for stitching label per shirt or pant or vest, kids will take it up as a competition to get as much of money as possible. How benifited the contractor would be!

In the match stick manufacturing factories and explosive shops of Shivakashi, more than fifty thousand kids earn their living. The rate of accidents here is alarming. In the coffee, tea and cardamom plantations of Kerala and Tamil Nadu, there is no statistics available for the number of child labourers.

In Kancheepuram, Tamil Nadu, more than 75 percent of the inhabitants are handloom workers. One third of the workers are kids. They work for about 10 hours a day. In Kerala, in most of the sea food companies are forced to work in the night. The fishermen bring fishes in the evening. Work starts by 4 pm and ends by 7 am. If they are studying, most of them are, think of the difficulty they face compromising both sleep and studies. This in turn have socio -

psychological and health related difficulties in them. Nobody seems to be bothered about them. No children's day celebration is indented for them.

In the metropolitan cities Mumbai and Kolkatha, the situation is still worse. Monthly remuneration for kids ranges from 60 to 120 and 15 to 50 respectively. But in comparison to African and sub-Saharan countries these kids are fortunate. There, kids work in fields of big land lords, with no remuneration. For this kids are beaten up mercilessly, nearly six to seven lakh kids work like this. At times kids get killed in beating, at times they end up in bed inflicted with they health issues. They are crippled right at the start of the life. They die a pitiable death. In South Africa, from a time span of 1976-1979 kids who showed lack of interest in work were arrested and put in jail. There, due to cruel beating up, lot of them died. The claim against them was that they disobeyed the African social policy.

What are the benefits of child labour? The wage is very meager, much lesser that an adult, but could extract as much work as possible. More than kids will not form unions and wage strike against the masters. All these are beneficial for the land lords and merchants.

It is not only poverty that compels kids to do labour, it is their parents ignorance and lack of consciousness and affection too. Even in our state there are situations where kids and wife remains unfed and hungry and the man of the house who earns the living drinking and lavishes his earnings. How many children's day we have celebrated after independence! We have even celebrated year for the child. When such a situation prevail and you do not realize there are children in such a desperate situation that you don't feel that it is a boon to be able to study and write exams. It is time that you understand the reality. You should know how to utilize such on opportunity. There is possibility that opportunities don't come in plenty. It is a rarity. So it is absolutely important to prepare well and take advantage of every situation to the fullest and due justice to oneself and the dear ones.

5
The parent's responsibility

In Order for the child to learn well and write the exam, there are some very specific responsibilities that the parent should take care of. They should be the best father and mother, purposefully. For this, some tips are mentioned below.

1. Never try to force things on kids. Don't ever enslave them. Let them grow as themselves. Each individual has his or her personality. Parents should try to enrich that and should try to better the personality, of the child not inhibit the growth. There is no need for reprim ending. Beating will not do any good; fear factor will not work always. But pampering and stuffing with love will also do not good.

2. Should kids be punished by beating? There are people who believe that kids should be punished. There are people who believe that kids should never be beaten. Both the approaches are wrong.

   All kids need not be punished. Many a times no punishment is needed. Just build an impression that if the child does anything unexpected of him /her as a student, he will be reprimanded. If the child becomes too disobedience, might be he deserves some punishment. But he should not be hurt for simple irritabilities of the parents. There are parents who hit their children just for their own faults. Some parents will make difficult the kids life just for falling a bit back in studies.

Rather than hitting kids for this thing and that thing ask them what compelled them to do that. Be empathetic. Consider their age and immaturity. Always have a positive approach rather than shouting for every fault. Always boost their confidence. Correct them when they go wrong. Give them a very patient hearing. Talk to them freely. If they repeat a mistake after frequent advices, then there should be some form of punishment. While one of the parents is scolding or punishing the child, the other one stands for the child then it will have severe negative consequences.

3. The environment inside the home should be peaceful. There should not be conflict and frequent fights between parents. Rather the relation with in the family should be loving, hearty and strong. This is absolutely necessary for a healthy environment conducive for study. There should be mutual respect between parents. They should support each other. Unity between parents is extremely essential for not only studies but also the well being of the children. Otherwise, kids will take undue advantage of the situation, form clicks within the family and ultimately it will result in worse results in examinations.

4. Whenever there are certain unrests within the family, it should not be permitted to grow. Either of the parents should take

control of the situation and handle it. Conflicts between kids should not be encouraged. It is natural that at times relations get strained. Head of the family has special responsibility in tacking the situation lightly and making things right. Parents with good humour skill could manage conflicts easily.

5. More than regulating the children, parents should be more concerned about their proper conduct in the family. Be role models. Do justice to whatever activity you engage, be trustworthy, and truthful. Avoid treachery of any form, for you are under constant surveillance by your children. All the virtues will add on to the success and wellbeing of the kids.

6. All the parents could not be immensely rich and influential. But all could be sensible and virtuous. Most difficult thing is to become humane. If that is possible for the parents, it will be easier for the kids to reach that perfection. They then, will win all the exams and hardships in life. It is not only enough to spend money for kids but is essential to give them opportunity and freedom to learn.

7. Many of the parents try to accomplish the peaceful life they had dreamed through their children.

8. It is absolutely foolish to control the kids beyond some extend. The misbehavior they show must be corrected and should be trained to be better individuals.

9. Kids should be encouraged while they prepare for exams. Their small achievements should be duly regarded and motivated.

10. While kids are preparing for exams they should have a very peaceful atmosphere. For this there should not be any conflict

of interest or quarrel between the parents. In the lower strata of society the pertinent issues are poverty and drunken parent. There are instances of constant quarrel in a lot of families which destroys the confidence and happiness of kids. Their fate is in the hands of the parents when they are young. That should not be put at stake.

Even in families belonging to upper strata, there will be some other instances of struggle and unhappiness. Money will not make any one happy. So it is essential to give peace of mind for a learning child.

6

Are exams a golden opportunity to victory?

We Keralites are much interested in foot ball. I had analyzed this fact seriously. This form of sports seems to be connected to our flow of life.

Just as in foot ball, there are chances for us to strike a goal, in every life there are equal chances for victory. In the sports event, all the hurdles placed by the opposite team is suitably handled by the player and opportunities to get goals are created. This is by the concerted effort of the team of players. This happens in both the teams and those who take advantage of the best effort will win the event. There would be instances where the best chances could not be converted as goal. There would be instances where the chances were less, but the utilization was par excellent so that victory is with that team. This is commonly happened with no exceptions.

This is applicable in our lives. In sports, there would be teams and captains and team mates to take care of the situation. But in life, we are the captain. We have to form strategies and fight alone. We have to wait for appropriate chances. These chances are the keys for victory in life. The issue is whether it is possible for the kid to make good use of the key and open the treasure of victory. But if the kid fails in the effort, the opportunity is lost and so is the effort taken.

Life also struggles in the fire of failure. The kid becomes desperately disappointed. This is the fate of the kid who spoils opportunity to learn well.

Hence it is absolutely necessary to make good use of each opportunity and all instances for the benefit of oneself and others. Be ready to do sacrifices for the same. Then victory will be yours. See the below example.

It happened quarter a century back. In my village, there was a feud between the dominant political parties of Kerala. 6 men were stabbed to death. That night I wishended over the interview letter from the Engineering College. You should remember that at that time, there was one and only one engineering college in the whole of Kerala. Number of seats was limited. It was extremely difficult to get an admission there. If I have to join, I had to start that night itself. Other wise I could not even dream of securing that admission or even appearing for the interview. The opportunity is lost forever.

My father lived in the present; he was not at all futuristic. Hence, there was no money for the travel. The situation was too worse to go out of the home for lending from some. That night was pitch black, the confusion and tension arose by the political feud was maximum. What to do? Fathers eyes were wet. Seeing the agony of such a strong man, I started crying and my mother was also weeping.

As if in trans father got up, went inside the home. He packed a pair of dress. There was half a sack of paddy which was kept as seed. He took it and placed on my head. Holding my hand, he ran in to the darkness. While I got tired, he held the sack, when he was tired, me. At the end we reached the small railway station. The train was ready to depart. Station master was wagging the green flag. We ran in to one of the boggy. After five hours, we reached a station. With the help of a kind porter, father sold the seed. With the small amount we got, we undertook an 18 hour journey in train. We reached the state capital Thiruvananthapuram, attended the interview, secured admission. Or else, my family would have remained in extreme poverty and dismay.

I wanted to highlight the fact that opportunity can be sometimes converted to golden opportunity only with an element of risk is taken. This will not only make sure victory but also brings in better opportunities. Life is an adventurous journey or experimentation. For this we have to think and work in a very large scale. Then only our activities become perfect. It is our dedication, selflessness and the element of risk that we take converts opportunity in to success.

Think about reading this article. If you are reading it for the sake of reading without getting the gist of it, it will only result in losing of your precious time. If you understand the idea but fail to utilize it, then also you are just wasting your time. But if the main idea becomes source of strength for your life and if you could make use of it practically, it becomes a real boon.

So, hence forth try to convert the golden opportunity, exams as a sources of strength of your life.

7

For prestigious victory in exams

A victory should be prestigious. For this there should some strategies of learning. What are they? For getting a clear answer, the author had conducted some interviews with some individuals who have made remarkable progress in life in terms of study. They have had great success in life too.

1. A student who succeeded in medical entrance exam with high score

I studied understanding the portion very well. It became handy for the entrance test.

2. An IAS officer

I used to study the lessons daily, even if I got tired. I used to read aloud, then would try to memorise by jotting the points down. I always based my studies on the prescribed text book. I used to go through a portion at least four times. I would prepare question answers. Essays were prepared in short form in small chits. Nearly 6 hours will be used for studies. I used to start at

5 am. I specially dedicated a portion of my time for reading news paper and for having food.

3. Another IAS officer

First I used to read a portion and then wrote it, difficult portions are re written. My studies were always oriented towards examination. I never had a stipulated time table, whenever I found it conducive for learning, I used to learn. When I felt like sleeping, I slept.

4. IIT graduate

Tried to know things and applied what all things I knew in a logical fashion.

5. A Doctor

I used to chant poems and formulas. Formulas were written down and pasted on wall. I also used to work out previous question papers regularly.

6. A Professor

I used to read news papers and articles. I had voracity towards reading. These enhanced my interest over studies. I used to have quizzes with my father. I used to prepare short notes on important part. Cross reference was also done so that my study became holistic and complete. I used to memorize a lot of quotations. No one ever compelled me to learn.

7. Another Professor

I used to learn lessons daily. That made me very confident. I concentrated on my studies more. This made me the most successful student in the class. I could decide things quickly.

Along with studies, I made friends. I was a voracious reader. My reading increased my memory. I had an enviable memory and could reproduce whatever I learned in appropriate context. I completed my lessons daily. I never kept my homework aside. For me studies were my way of self actualization. And examination is faced by a lot of people at a time. My confidence was my strength. I used to concentrate well when taught.

8. A Rank holder

Daily I used to allote an average of 5 to 6 hours for study. I used to wake up very early in the morning and read. Then I would think about what I read. I also prepared answers for the questions most expected to be asked in the exam.

9. A student who secured first rank for SSLC exam

More than learning only the prescribed curriculum, I used to read a lot on general awareness and out of curriculum.

10. A graduate rank holder

I never had any specific plan of action. Whenever I felt like studying, I used to study well. I used to mark the relevant textual portions. I took notes and studied them well. For exams, I read through these short notes. I never stayed late in the night. Rather I slept a bit early and woke up pretty early. Early morning was very conducive for my studies. I was not very particular in finishing off the daily lessons, but made sure to complete the portion for exams on time. I never did any gambling with studies. Along with my studies, I concentrated in poetry and prose writing, music etc. All these activities kept me in good spirits and made my studies easy and interesting.

11. A girl who secured rank in Post Graduation

I used to listen in the class and learned my daily lessons. So exam was never a nightmare for me. I learnt for only 4 hours a day. My experience is that there is no need to learn 27 x 7, but when you learn, learn with all the might. Once I joined for my P G programme, I had to change my learning style. Long essays were prepared by me. At times, I could not complete my learning in the same day. But I used to prepare short notes of the essays I prepared. Since I had byhearted them, exam was never an issue for me.

12. Rank holder for a competetive exam

I never studied hard right at the start of the academic year. But before exam, for 3 months I did work in a much disciplined manner. I made time tables for each subject; time is allotted according to the importance of the subject and its difficulty. According to me for students of arts subject, study leave is extremely important.

But for science subjects, ideal way is to write and learn rather than just reading through. Since I had adopted this as my strategy, learning was never a difficulty for me. I listened very well in the class. Even though I was not up to date, I made good use of my study leave. The systematic way of learning was the one the enabled me to be a winner.

But when you concentrate only on the revision holidays, it is extremely difficult to prioritise the subjects property. You should be very cautious. The available time should be properly apportioned. For each day there should be a timetable. There should be review and follow up. If some unforeseen things happen, you will have to make good the rest of the time. When you learn the important ideas should be written down and learned by heart. One way of remembering the important points is by repeatedly learning them just before going to bed and memorizing the same when you wake up early in the morning.

See the different ways of learning adopted different winners, all are winners but they have their own style of learning which have made them successful. There are some common areas of agreement by the majority, but individual differences are there. It is for each child to develop a pertinent learning habit for his/her own. You can adopt any combination of the above methods as per your choice and suitability.

8
Practical Ways of Making Study More Effective

1. If you feel any kind of physical constraints such as headache, low eye sight, etc, get those corrected at once.
2. Choose a specific place for learning.
3. Remove all the substances which would distract your attention or impede your learning
4. Plan your learning
5. Never compromise with sleep in the days of examinations, it will lead to ill health
6. Never mug up. Understand before you memorize.
7. Take a stock of most probable questions, prepare answers and learn.
8. Don't take long break between studies
9. Learn sequentially.
10. Learn difficult spellings byheart. This is extremely important while you learn a language.
11. Make short noting for long essays.
12. Graphical representation, pictures etc. are to be learned along with the chapter concerned.
13. Never lose your heart or courage while you are learning.
14. Never fear exams un necessarily.

9

Will poverty impede learning? How will the kids who are forced to work find time for studies? Are there any tips?

They have to be stronger, they will be devoid of any creature comforts, will not have any time left for play. But the labour that they take for excelling in studies will surely be rewarded. They will reap better result and will be able to give a better life to their next generation.

Sure, they will get only nominal time than the other kids. But they could find some better ways for adapting to the situation. While body is devoted to work, they can think about their studies. They can make mental revision of things they have byhareated. They can introspect things like how far the portions has been studied, which portion remains, what are the doubts, which all portions are difficult etc. This is as good as a revision.

10

Rich parents send their kids to courses which they are least interested. What would be the result? Will they succeed?

If we send kids to courses which they dislike, learning becomes a headache. They will get disappointed. They may even develop depression.

This is Ramakrishna's real life story:

I became warden of a college hostel when I was very young. There were 300 inhabitants. I wanted to do justice towards my job and so I tried many approaches towards managing the students. I had the role of a father who wanted to make his son bettered. At times I also took the role of a strict guardian who could both punish and protect. Then I behaved like a best friend with whom any one would find a solution for any of their issues. This way the role of my liking. This role suited me most and was beneficial for the students. By this, I could understand the real self of the so called naughty and rebellious kids. Otherwise, I understood Ramakrishna better in my mentor's role.

Ramakrishna was a rebellious boy. Within a year, he was noticed by all the teachers in a totally negative manner. Teachers hated him for his vices. One day his math's lecturer fainted in the lecture hall. She was taking attendance. Once she took the roll, as soon as Ramakrishna's name was called, from inside the draw, a blast was heard. It was a programme planned and executed by our Ramakrishna. A small explosive was lit and kept inside the desk so that at a time he desire it would explode and make havoc.

Another day was just dawn and I wake up hearing a blood curdling cry from within the hostel toilet. When I ran towards the toilet complex, a room was locked from outside. I opened the door and let that boy out. I could easily identify the culprit. Who else would do such bitter comedy? I went to his room. Ramakrishna was mimicking a sleep. I asked him to follow me to the warden's room. He came along. He opened up his mind to me. I could soon pin down his issue. He was an intelligent student, but was not interested in conventional methods of learning. His inclination was towards electrical and electronic activities. When he was in high school, he used to do wiring of households. His skill and in born trait would have made him an excellent electrician. That was his dream. But his parents who were senior government offices and his brother who was an engineer despised his plans. Thus he was sent to the college. It was as difficult for him as he was pushed in to deep sea.

To avoid these difficulties there should be a proper introspection from the part of all about which branch of study suits the kid. The child's interest should be asked. When we impose our likes on the child, due to respect and love he/she might not disagree. Eventually, their disagreement my surface on a later point of time in a disruptive manner. It may be self destructive, also. So, whatever the parent has done with the belief that it is best for the child will become utter foolishness. To deal with such situation properly, there should be changes in the admission criteria of colleges. Either swim or drown and die should not be the criteria. Opportunity for the student to evaluate oneself should be available. He/she should know what the purpose of education is. Before pushing one to deep sea, he may be taught swimming in a pool. From this we could understand his innate sense, taste, and interest in a particular subject. One the basis of these should be choice of his subject. Then there will not be cases like Ramakrishna.

11

Are there any techniques for getting better marks?

Yes. There are. It does not matter how much you know. What matter is how you apply the information will you in the required time frame. To secure maximum marks in exam, proper training is a must. Collect all the previous question papers. Prepare answer corresponding to them. Later, answer the question paper as if you write a real exam. Time should be kept. For this, timepiece should be used. Training will help you to keep pace. Effort should be taken so that in minimum time, maximum questions could be attempted. This type of training would be beneficial for writing the examination perfectly. Repeat learning would facilitate better marks in the exam.

12

How to improve your speed of learning while preparing for exam

When you are doing your final preparation, you should be very agile. You should grasp things within a short span of time. For making this possible, you should have learnt your daily lessons. You should read well, but should practice controlled reading. You should be thorough enough with the portions so that you need to glance through the portion and find out the most important ones and read that portion alone thoroughly. For that you have to know precisely what should be learned. Questions should be framed on the basis of importance. Your reading should be focusing the answers for the questions. Then your thought would be in the right direction. Otherwise, your mind will roam around unnecessary things and learning becomes shallow.

How to plan for exam based study?

When a new academic year starts itself should start the preparation for learning. Food, travel, sleep, household chores, routine lecture, practical classes etc., should be provided separate time. The rest of the time should be dedicated for rest and enjoyment. Likewise, 168 hours of a week should be properly utilized. A format for use is could be as below. The timing could be customized according to individual needs.

Time	Monday	Tuesday	Wednesday	Thursday	Friday	Saturday	Sunday
7. 00 am							
8.00 am							
9.00 am							
10.00 am							
11.00 am							
12.00 noon							
1.00 pm							
2.00 pm							
3.00 pm							
4.00 pm							

5.00 pm
____
6.00 pm
____
7.00 pm
____
8.00 pm
____
9.00 pm
____
10.00 pm

14

Is examination essential?

1. Why examination

   In responsible positions, the one who is eligible should be placed. For this, there should be exam. For any job, if there is a qualifying exam, that will reduce the chance of bribe and corruption. Examination is an indication of quality of teaching. If there is an exam the student will become more responsible. While preparing for an exam the student could understand the depth and extend of a subject. One could get an understanding about his strength and weakness in a particular substance. A teacher could also understand the appropriateness of his teaching skills and knowledge in the substance.

2. Is an exam an appropriate criterion to examine the intelligence and skill of a student?

   No, it is not. But no one has found out any other better criteria for an evaluation. Hence students have to prepare well for any exam.

3. Is it good to persuade the child to study?

   No. Control and advice beyond a limit is detrimental to the child. If a child is thrashed and controlled beyond an extend, even if it is for maintaining discipline or to better his/her studies, there is every possibility that it would result in making him/her mentally wreck. There is no need to trust upon once belief or values extensively in one's own kids. But a parent should for sure show the path. They should expose their children on the rightness of things. If we compel, child is sure to deviate from the path.

4.   Most probable questions.

Let it be any type of exam, exams conducted by government for the prospective employees, competitive exams, university exams, or scholarship exams, on a close observation, it is felt that the questions can be typified in to two.

In the first type, the questions are specifically logical. For such questions there could only be one answer. Whoever attempts this question should get the same answer. Multiple choice questions, yes or no type questions, fill up as appropriate type questions; arithmetic etc falls under this category.

The second type is more subjective and generic. There is no one single answer for such questions. If a question ask us to Explain, illustrate, examine, analyze, describe, relate, criticize, comprehend or elucidate, such questions can be written on the basis of your expertise. Each student could approach that question in their own way.

15

When you really start learning

1. One should explore the importance of each exam. There is no merit in just appearing for an exam like S S L C and getting a pass mark. If one find it difficult to do justice in an year then wait for the next exam, write with ample preparation and write it in the second chance. But the student should be very much sure of this. All the future prospect of a student is based on his SSLC mark. It is the basis of any job which he would secure in the due course.

2. He/She should be aware of the time available and the probable number of questions.

3. Type of questions. Whether logical, technical or generic.

4. Which all materials can be taken into the exam hall such as mathematical tables, calculators, drinking water etc.

5. Tools to be taken in like scale, instruments etc.,

6. Extend of a portion depicted in the syllabus. Whether all the chapters are included for the examination or not.

How to fetch better marks

You should study very scientifically and systematically. Fully concentrate in the subject. Along with your personal preparation, daily lessons taught in the class should also be learned. Enlist the most probable questions. Write answers accordingly. This experience will help you in writing the examination:

Is it ok to byheart portions?

We have heard of arguements that it is not proper to byheart lessons. But this opinion cannot be generalized to all students and all subjects. It is dependent on the opportunity that a student gets for his studies and the real situation in which he undertakes his study. A poor student who is not conversant with the subject and who is not able to take the support of an external resource, at times, will have to study portions byheart. This is essential for him/her as the overall performance of a student is rated on the basis of the marks he receives. He has to secure a minimum mark for his difficult subject too. Likewise, formulas, poems, equations, quotations etc., are to be learned byheart. But one should know what is the idea or concept behind the portion which is learned.

When the languages are learned, what all things should be taken care of?

When you learn languages like English, French, Sanskrit, Malayalam, Hindi, Tamil, Kannada etc., spelling of words should be learned properly. Difficult words are to be written down. To get the real meaning of important words, use them to make sentences of your own. Along with reading and memorizing, important points should be tested by writing them down. The poetry that you have memorized should also be written and seen that the punctuations are ok.

Points to be noted while you learn science subjects

Diagram's and pictures are of great importance. While you learn you may feel that just by seeing and visualizing you will be able to recreate a picture in the exam paper. But when you really attempt, you will be in great difficulty. You will lose your precious time and mark as well. Hence make sure you draw and redraw till the thing remains in your heart and brain. Mostly if a answer is re instated by a figure, it will get good marks. In a question where diagrams are needed along with the answer part, teachers give you mark on the evaluation of the picture.

Points to be noted while you learn mathematics

There are several major things you have to take care of. Maths can never be learnt by looking at the textual portion or by reading and by hearing. You have to actually work out a problem. You have to find out the easy and simplest way towards an answer. All the equipments in the instrument box should be understood and used well. Formulas and equations are to be learnt byheart. Principles are to be understood well. You should make your handwriting more clear. Working column should be maintained properly. When you take out an answer from working column and put it on the answer sheet care should be taken not to create mistakes.

Tips for learning social science subjects better

When you learn history, bare in mind that you are learning a story which has taken place in the society years before. Relate the story with time frame and read it well. Relate it with some instances of the present day. Dates and years are to be byhearted. When you learn geography your imagination would help you. Visualize the land forms, flora and fauna. Imagine that you are physically present there. Then you will better understand the climatic conditions, earth, soil and other resources. You will be able to internalize the culture and art forms.

What is the single tip which would help a student excel both in studies and exam?

His/her ability to concentrate.

16
How to concentrate?

I can 't concentrate is a plea heard everywhere. The power to concentrate is so worthy to possess. How can this be gained?

1. Lead a pious life

For this, figure out your faults. Never try to find fault with others. Reduce the wrong happenings in life. By this, life will become more attractive and success. Thus you can lead a pious life.

2. Learn self control

In daily life interactions, there is some self control which we have to exercise. We have to have some restriction over our life. For example, food, sleep, viewing things, etc. Read only good literature. Don't go for the bad ones. For example, avoid bad books, bad movies etc. Never use negative words or things. Control all your sense organs. This is the art of self control.

Your views and vision should be clear. If we become doubtful and unclear, we will not be able to see the truth. A doubtful person can never concentrate and exercise self control. Fear also kills concentration. Hence never be doubtful. As browning has pointed out, god is there at the heaven, ad here at earth thinks will be alright.

3. Always fill your mind the best of the emotions and thoughts.

17
Dealing with exam

1. How could it be possible to present questions in an exam?

   While learning, prepare model questions and attempt writing answers to it.

2. How exam and the future of one who write the exam are mutually related?

   Exam is a balance which weighs one's life. That is the reason why people get tensed while exam comes.

3. How can we reduce or control the tension.

   It is very difficult to completely avoid tension. But there are ways in which this can be controlled. One of the best ways in this regard is to be prepared for the exam with maximum care.

4. How should you deal with exam

   We should make friends with exam don't detest it. If you are starting to drown, is there any point in struggling with it? Rather show interest on it so that you will naturally found some way to get away from it. Hence show maximum interest in examinations.

5. Things to be kept in mind when you write an exam.

    First attempt the easiest questions. I will tell you why it is important. Imagine there are 2 parts for a question paper and there are four questions in the second part. Time available is one hour. A student reads the question. He feels he is confident with the last 3 questions but not very sure about the first one. But the first question, Since it comes first he attempts first as it was the practice. Since he was doubtful, he had to spend at least 25 minutes in thinking and analyzing the question. Still he was not able to find and answer and he struggled for further more. He realized his folly only after 45 minutes. He got nervous; he is yet to finish the first question. The rest four is also to be answered . He tried to do something but ended up in utter failure.

    That is why it is always advisable to attempt the easy question first. First pick the ripe apple and put it in the basket. You will gain so much of confidence that you will even be able to make doubtful questions right.

6. It is natural for a candidate to get nervous in an exam hall and when he gets the question paper. Can it be controlled?

    Be confident. You have learned well so there is no need to be afraid. Tell this to your mind repeatedly. Comfort it and strengthen it.

    If you have out of syllabus questions asked, you have to tell yourself that it requires no great knowledge in asking tough questions which even a bright student can't answer, but you can surely reach the answer if you could think properly. Then think on the basis or related portions which you have learnt. Be calm and you will derive at the proper answer.

7. How can you make good of each second you get in the exam hall? What are the challenges that you face an exam hall? How can you equip yourself for that?

a) Reach the exam hall at the earliest. Find out the seating dedicated to your role number. Get yourself seated. Then never try to get yourself in to difficult thoughts. Keep cool. Never think negative. Don't interact, make merry or quarrel with others. While you try to memorize, if you feel like you have forgotten things, don't panic. Think positive. If you are a believer, pray, if you are not, try to mediate. Tell yourself that you are going to write the exam well. Tell yourself that you are going to secure good marks.

b) Fear is like fire, it burns. It spreads very fast. So if there are questions which you don't know, please keep calm. Condition yourself that if such a question or a question from a portion not taught is asked, I will think and find out an answer. Arrange your answer systematically from whatever you know. Challenge back this challenge. Don't get disheartened.

c) Even if you fail in getting the answer, don't copy from others. Even if you get some answer, your tension will not permit you to write it right. It is unethical. It will kill your future. You will be debarred from writing further exams.

d) When you get the question paper, don't waste your time in repeatedly reading the questions. Just scan the question paper once. Ascertain the number of questions and apportioning of marks. Calculate time to be devoted to different questions. Once you do this, start writing the exam.

e) When you are writing an essay, as you complete couple of pages, read and do the correction. For short answers, complete the section and check. Likewise correct what you have written intermittently. Then at the end you will have to make correction of only few pages of your answer sheets. And by clubbing checking with writing, your hand gets some rest. Your mind gets fresh. It will help you write the next answer more clearly and compactly.

f)   When it is the case of multiple choice questions, you can attempt it first. While you read the question you can write the answer. If you have doubt, read the question again. Then you might be able to get the right answer.

For exmple see the question.

What is the instrument used to measure eclectic current?

a)   Volt meter

b)   Ammeter

c)   Watt meter

d)   Ohm meter

If you feel that three of them are wrong you can go for the other. The answer will be correct. If you are not totally sure, you can always make a sensible assumption. But the student should have at least an idea about the portion dealt with.

For example.

The paper mill of Kollam district is situated at

a)   Velloor

b)   Kalloor

c)   Amballor

d)   Punalur

Here the student should have basic information about the district. He should know that 3 of the places ie, Velloor, kalloor and Amballor are not part of Kollam district. Then only his choice would be right.

When you right answer to multiple choice questions, you should follow the instructions closely. In most of the western countries for such problems evaluation is done by the machines. If instructions are not followed the machines will not give marks. Same situation is there here is various competitive examinations.

There are some complications with multiple choice questions. Some students will not be able to comprehend the question properly.

Here is an example

Fill up the blank with a number

$$4 \div \underline{\quad} = \underline{\quad} \div 16$$

The answer is 8

If you replace the blank portion by x, it would be easy

$4 \div x = x \div 16$

$4/x = x/16$

Therefore, $4x^2 = 64$

$X = 8$

At times students will not see both the blanks due to tension. Hence there is more probability for them to make mistakes. Hence read the question properly.

For a question, all the choices should be analyzed.

For example

All human being wear

a)   Pants

b)   Shirt

c)   Shoes

d)   Clothes

Here the right answer is clothes. There is a possibility that the moment you see the first option, that will be chosen. Never get prejudiced.

See this question.

A van is costly than a jeep. A van is less costly than a scooter. If this is so, what is most costly?

a) Van

b) Jeep

c) Scooter.

Your commonsense may mislead you here. You may opt for van, but according to this question the answer is scooter. The question is out of the answers given, for the question what the answer is. To avoid such confusion, read the question and answer again.

g) You should manage your time properly. You should be time conscious.

h) Answer all the questions. Limit the size of answer. Don't repeat the statements you have made. It may irritate the examiner. You may lose marks. Clarity of answer and brevity are very important.

i) Answer sheets should be serially numbered. This should be done as soon as you get the main and additional sheets. Don't wait for the exam to get over. You may misplace the paper and my tie it in utter disorder. Tying up should also be proper. If you lump up the tie, the evaluator may feel embarrassed on you lack of interest and you may lose marks.

j) When you write the answer, high light the salient points by underlining. Pictures should be drawn clearly. When you take the answers from working column and write it in main sheet, don't make silly mistakes.

k)   Math problems should be done with greater concentration.

l)   Except for multiple choice questions, it is advisable to spend a minute in reading the question and planning and structuring the answer.

There can be more than hundred suggestions for improving you approach towards exam and answering a question paper. But responsibility rests with the one who write the exam. Each second should be made used of. Mind and health should be in equilibrium. You should be contented and your mind should be fearless. You should be having better concentration. For this, the training should happen long before the actual exam.

18
What is an interview?

1. What does it mean?

    Interview is an English word. The word is derived from two words from French language Entre, and Volre. It means directly in detail. Whether a person is suitable for a particular job, a course, a certification or a particular degree is ascertained by a face to face interaction with the candidate. This is interview.

2. What should be your attire for an interview?

    The dressing up should befit the job you are aspiring for. For an engineer, mechanic, overseer, skilled worker etc. pants and shirt would suit. For a teacher, formal wear should be opted for. For an artist, showy type dress would suit. Your dress should be clean and well pressed. Don't use glaring bright colours.

    If you are a habitual dhoti wearer, make sure you start practising wearing pants a week before the interview.

    Undergarments should be neat and clean. Socks should not be torn. Shoes should be polished. Don't use heavy perfume. Make sure, you reach the place at least half an hour prior to the interview.

3. Is there any difference between an interview and the viva voce which is conducted after a theory exam?

Viva voce is a Latin phrase literally meaning "with living voice" but most often translated as "by word of mouth." Here, after a theory or a practical examination, oral questions are asked. This is a kind of interview. It is not the physical appearance or appeal of a person that is rated in a viva voce, but the general awareness of the candidate on a specific subject, body language, way of behaviour and attitude will be rated.

4.   How to get ready for an interview

You should have a detailed knowledge on the specific area specialization, the job to which you are trained to, general knowledge, national and international affairs, and areas of current importance from which questions would be asked. In an interview, attempt will be there to understand the character of the candidate. For this there will be enquiry on your hobby. Be prepared to answer.

5.   Regarding general knowledge and current affairs, important dates and events are to be memorized. Regarding modern events, questions will be limited to the time span of two years.

6.   Things that should be taken along for an interview.

Certificates in original should be with you. It should be properly indexed and kept so that you can produce it when it is needed. There is no need for cooling glass, bag, umbrella, pencil etc in the site of interview. Don't keep unnecessary things in the table before the interviewers. They may feel uneasy about such behaviours.

7.   How to keep calm during an interview.

Once you enter the room, take a deep breath. Think about happy occurrences. Imagine that you are going to qualify the interview. Communicate with the other candidates. Drink lot of water. Most importantly, smile.

8.   How to salute the interviewers?

You can either fold your hand in respect or say a wish as per the time. Bow your head slightly. If they ask you to sit, sit comfortably leaning to the backrest. Don't bite your nails or pull off your hair. Don't fold the tip of the shirt or sari. If you don't know an answer, politely say so. Keep eye contact. Never impose or question. Never put on unnecessary hallow.

9. How should you answer?
    Be loud enough
    Pronunciation should be proper
    Don't utter monosyllables. Answer in a complete sentence.
    Never impose yourself.
    Don't mumble
    Don't be over humble
    Never argue, if you have a different point to rise, do it politely and pleasantly

10. How should you wind up your interview?
    Thank them, take your certificates, go out of the room without turning back.

19
Failure in exam

Why did they fail in the exam? What is to be done with the one who failed?

This is true story; There is an old traditional family. House is very old and its physical condition is deplorable. On its veranda, there sits a boy, hiding his head in to his lap. He failed for the S S L C examination. He is one among those unfortunate thousands.

As usual, this year also the exam result was announced. Media covered the success stories. The victors were all interviewed. News paper wrote cover stories on likes, dislikes and merits of those who made a mark. This has become a common practice and there is nothing wrong in it. But as always, now also we fail to understand the reasons of failure and those who have failed. I wanted to change this game. So I observed that boy in detail. A very lean structure, his dress was not clean, hair unkempt. He was in deep thought, in agony and permit. As if in a dream, he collected pebbles from the ground and threw it up. I tried to analyze him. Then I understood how he failed. The house was in a very deplorable condition. He was the eldest in a family where the parents were constantly struggling. He had 6 siblings. When it is rainy season, poverty becomes deeper. One or other of his sibling will be ill. When he sees the agony in his mothers face, he will run to the hospital.

There are days which he wakes up with his father's alert. Father would say, "da, go to Mr……. That is for asking some loan against the agricultural produce which is yet to ripe. The prize will be very low. His home was always in indebtedness. There was no enough money for food, many a times he will not be able to buy all his text books. They had some cultivatable land. On sowing and reaping season, along with other workers, he would also do the labour. Then he would miss the class.

When it is sunny and dry, the responsibility of watering the field is his. He wakes up early morning, feeds the cattle and rust to the field. By 11, watering gets over. He rushes back at home, take a bath and proceeds to school. He is sure to be late. He will be made fun of by the teacher and his classmates. He would be scolded and at times beaten up. At home, every evening, father comes back getting drunk. He ill treats the family, beats up his wife and kids. The family was in constant agony.

I felt like seeing a bud which is not permitted to grow, which is nibbled untimely. When his environment is such cruel and unfriendly how can I pacify him? But I wanted to make him comfortable, I asked him.

Which subject did you fail?

"English"

Then which subject is difficult for you?

"Hindi"

I struggled to continue the discussion. Might be, he understood my discomfort, and continued the conversation.

"My father wants me to learn and to get a good job. He has promised me a study leave for 3 months. If so I will win. I have none other than god to help me. I have to win; I have to win for my family. I will succeed."

I was amazed to see his self confidence. I wished him good luck. Let his confidence make him a winner.

But such confidence is lacking in most of the kinds who have the same family background. One should not fear the life but have to embrace it fondly. Once should go ahead, alone, at times.

Will all the poor and vulnerable fail in life? Will all the well of always win. No, it is not so. This is the story of Sreelatha.

Sreelatha comes from a well off family, father, a business man, mother, teacher and elder brother works with a bank. There is no financial constraint. But the girl is least interested in studies. She is just interested in expressing herself as a beautiful girl, would clad herself in costly attire and makeup. She reads about beauty tips as advised by film stars and models. She is always bothered about one beauty issue or the other.

"As soon as I hold the book for studies, I feel like sleeping," she claims.

"But how did you reach up to the 10th class?" I asked.

The girl giggled. I felt that her mischievous laughter was right on the face of our all past system in education. Now, up to 10th class you need not fear exam due to the "all pass" system

There are a lot of different reasons for the failure of different students. But all are suffers in one form or the other. Human life is so unpredictable and uncertain. What will happen if you place a mustard seed over the sharp rim of a vessel? It may fall at any time. It is just luck that it could say safe. It is very much like a lottery or rather a flying trapeze. A slight mistake will make you fall. Even though human beings have progressed; our life still is not secure. There is no point in blaming fate for something bad that is happening in our life. Such an argument that fate is responsible for our failure is just a trick of our mind and escapism. We can very well decide our destiny. Out acts control our fate. Our deeds control our fate. We should be able to control ourselves, but you have to try for that.

Have you ever walked through a reasonable distance through your own native place, be it urban or rural? Have you travelled through levelled and dirt road? While strolling, have you ever thought about it geography? There is an upheaval, a downhill, a field, a canal, a small bridge etc. This is the replica of our life. There are upheavals and downhills in life. It is as natural as the occurrence of day and night. But most of us linger in the dark and believe that it would last forever. They just struggle and lament. They never think that for this uphill surely there would be a valley.

Life is a journey which has to be traversed. When you travel for long in paths unknown, necessarily there would be situations where you may fall down. It is natural justice. Fearing a fall or anticipating it, can we stop walking? Then where is life in it? Life is dynamic, it is necessary that we move on. Static nature depicts death.

Have you fallen at least once in this journey of life? You should have, I am sure. And you stood up and walked again, did not you? But all are not like that. They will remain there and wail. No one will attend to them. At times people may get irritated. Never look forward for somebody's sympathy. They may detest you. The need of the day would be introspection, self criticism and self respect. The one who can hold you forward is yourself. Understand and unleash that power in you. We have to internalize the fact that we our self are our best friend and toughest foe. Try to get up. Try to be friend yourself. Grab that power. The physical strength would come from our mental power. Strength can be converted from one form to the other. That is nature's law.

How can this be possible? How to measure your mental strength? How can we process and convert our mental power to a physical power which would aid us to overcome our difficulties and march forward? Or how can we attain the mental strength which is the most powerful of the treasures available with us? For these varied questions, answers can be obtained from the lives of other people and our own life experiences. Experience matters.

In life, successes and failure are both natural, or it is the rule of law. When success motivates us, failure destroys our morale. Some of us never come out of the strong embrace of failure. They go slowly in to isolation and self destruction. But there is a hand full that, like a phoenix bird, rises from their own ashes. They gallop into the victory stand. There life progresses.

Imagine you fall in the seamless water. If you have self confidence, even when you start breathless and fears drowning, you will be searching for at least a hay stalk to hold and to escape. At any cost you will try to get away from the water. You may struggle so hard so that at the end you may learn swimming. You may otherwise cry aloud so that someone would hear you and may help you out of the water. You may even find some sort of mechanism were you get away. But a person who is very meek and fearful will die out of fright. While a coward dies of fright even before his actual death, and a brave one get over death even from its face. When I think about self confidence, let me reiterate my own experience. At that time, after school final the next step is to join intermediate at the college.

I was born in a very poor family. Our parental home, at the time of my teen age was almost under destruction. But I tried my best and won my tenth class. A person aquainted to my father heard about me, he was willing to help me continue my studies. This was solely on the basis of some favour which my father did for him during the past. He promised me that I can stay with his family and study. The same year, his son also joined that college. We became colleagues. I never expected any foul intention. But unfortunately the family made me their servant. I was regularly beaten up by the boy. I could not learn a thing and naturally I failed. All others blamed me. They thought me to be a big fool. I was sent out from home. I was literally orphaned. I had to leave my home.

My failure burned me. I was shattered. But my self-confidence awoke. I did introspection, analyzed my strengths and weaknesses. I found out where I went wrong. I was willing to correct me. I wanted to win. For my existence I had started taking up the job of porter. I never had a friend, cloths or a place to stay. I used to spend my nights in the railway platform. With nobody to help, I promised I will learn myself. I prepared a plan. During day time I worked. At night, up to midnight I made use of street light for my studies. I wrote the September examination. I desperately waited for the result. One day I saw that news in a Malayalam news paper. Butterflies started roaming inside my stomach, I was tensed. During those days Madras University conducted examination in the Trichur area. So the news paper from Thrichur, had only the result of Trichur area, which was very small in number.

I searched for my number in third class; it was not there, then in second class, then in the list of those won only the part. No, I was not there. I became dizzy, felt like I would fall down. But then I felt, I will never fail. My mind and conscience strengthened me. Gathering courage, I took the news paper again. There, my number was in there alone in the portion for candidates who received first class. I was the sole student who secured first class. I was over whelmed. I thanked god with all my might.

Afterwards I wrote a lot of exams. But the agony and emotions that ruled the intermediate exam still remains with me. I won only because of my confidence.

Failure need not be in exam. It could be in business, industry, human relation or any other areas. Where ever you fail, irrespective of its intensity gain your courage and confidence. Find out why you failed. If you identify the reason, you will surely find out ways towards victory. Believe that you are a winner. Even in dreams chant that you are going to win. Confidence is the shield, fear is our foe. So today you decide that you are going to win every exam in flying colours.